For Matthew, with love and laughter. — A.B.
For Lilian, Menno and Hanna, with love. — L.M.

OXFORD
UNIVERSITY PRESS

Great Clarendon Street, Oxford OX2 6DP

Oxford University Press is a department of the University of Oxford.
It furthers the University's objective of excellence in research, scholarship,
and education by publishing worldwide in

Oxford New York
Auckland Cape Town Dar es Salaam Hong Kong Karachi
Kuala Lumpur Madrid Melbourne Mexico City Nairobi
New Delhi Shanghai Taipei Toronto

With offices in
Argentina Austria Brazil Chile Czech Republic France Greece
Guatemala Hungary Italy Japan Poland Portugal Singapore
South Korea Switzerland Thailand Turkey Ukraine Vietnam

Oxford is a registered trade mark of Oxford University Press
in the UK and in certain other countries

British Library Cataloguing in Publication Data available

ISBN: 978-0-19-272985-9 (Hardback)
ISBN: 978-0-19-272986-6 (Paperback)

10 9 8 7 6 5 4 3 2 1

Printed in China

Paper used in the production of this book is a natural, recyclable product made
from wood grown in sustainable forests. The manufacturing process conforms to the
environmental regulations of the country of origin

Bug and Bear

Ann Bonwill & Layn Marlow

OXFORD
UNIVERSITY PRESS

Bug was being annoying.
He zipped and zapped around Bear's head.

'Will you play with me, Bear?' he buzzed. 'Please, please, pleazzzze?'

Bear didn't want to play. She wanted to nap.

'No, Bug,'
said Bear.
'I'm too tired
to play.'

She let out a big yawn and lumbered off
towards her cave. But Bug followed her,
buzzing all the way.

When Bear heard Bug buzzing
behind her, she lumbered
faster. So Bug buzzed faster.

'Chase!' said Bug.

'Is that what we're playing?'

'Not now, Bug,' said Bear.
'Oh,' said Bug. 'How about now?'
'Humph,' said Bear and kept on lumbering.

Bug stopped to smell some flowers.
He counted to ten.
'Maybe Bear wants to play now,'
he thought. So off he buzzed to find her.

'Double humph,' said Bear when she heard
Bug buzzing behind her again.
She lumbered faster
and faster . . .

so fast that she nearly
tripped over Chameleon
who was hiding in the
yellow leaves.

Chameleon gave Bear an idea. She would hide from Bug! She leaned against a tree, thinking brown thoughts. But Bear didn't blend into the bark as well as she'd hoped . . .

and along came Bug,
who spotted her
straight away.

'Hide and seek!' said Bug,

'Is that what we're playing?'

'Go away, Bug,' said Bear.
'I want to be alone.'

'We can be alone together!' said Bug.

'That's impossible,' said Bear.

'Oh,' said Bug.

When Bear grumped
past Tortoise,

he tucked into his shell
to keep out of her way.

Tortoise gave
Bear an idea.

She would crawl inside
a hollow log to keep
out of Bug's way.

But Bear couldn't quite squeeze all of herself in . . .
and Bug could recognize Bear's paws anywhere.

'Follow the leader!' said Bug.

'Is that what we're playing?'

'No, Bug,' said Bear.
'We are NOT playing.'

'Oh,' said Bug.

Just outside Bear's cave, Gecko was sunning
herself on a stone, sitting perfectly still.

Gecko gave
Bear an idea.

She stood stock still so that
Bug wouldn't notice her.

Her nose
was still.

Her arms
were still.

Even her ears
were still.

But Bear's eyelids were not still . . .

they were droopy.

'Statues!' said Bug.

'Is that what we're playing?'

'Buzz off, Bug!' said Bear.
'Go and jump in a lake!'

And with that she humphed into her cave.
This time Bug did not buzz after Bear.

'Quiet at last,' thought Bear,
as she settled down for her nap.

But Bear could not fall asleep.
She tossed and turned.

She tried counting squirrels.
Still she could not fall asleep.

'Maybe I should have been
nicer to Bug,' she thought.

So she went outside to find him.

'I'm ready to play now, Bug,' said Bear.

But Bug was not there. Bug was not anywhere.
No one had seen him—not Gecko, not Tortoise,
not Chameleon. He was nowhere to be found,
and Bear was **very** worried.

'Bug is my very best friend,' said Bear.
'I need to find him!'
'Maybe he went to the lake,' said Gecko.
'Just like you told him to,' said Chameleon.
Tortoise nodded wisely.

But he didn't like being a water bug,
And he wanted to come ashore.

Bear raced off to the lake and, sure enough,
there was Bug, floating on a lily pad.

Bear jumped into the water.

She huffed and puffed her way to the middle
of the lake, scooped Bug up in her paw,
and placed him on top of her head.

'I'm sorry, Bug,' said Bear,
when they were back on dry land.
'I shouldn't have said those mean things
to you. You are my very best friend.
Would you like to play now?'

'I'm too tired to play,' said Bug,
shaking the water from his wings.
'I think I'd like to have a nap.'

And so they did.
Together.